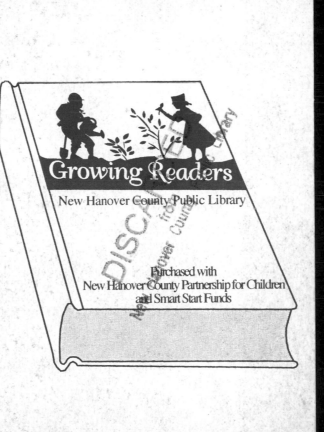

Whistling

STORY BY
Elizabeth Partridge

QUILTS BY
Anna Grossnickle Hines

Greenwillow Books
An Imprint of HarperCollinsPublishers

"Jake," Daddy whispers. "It's almost time."

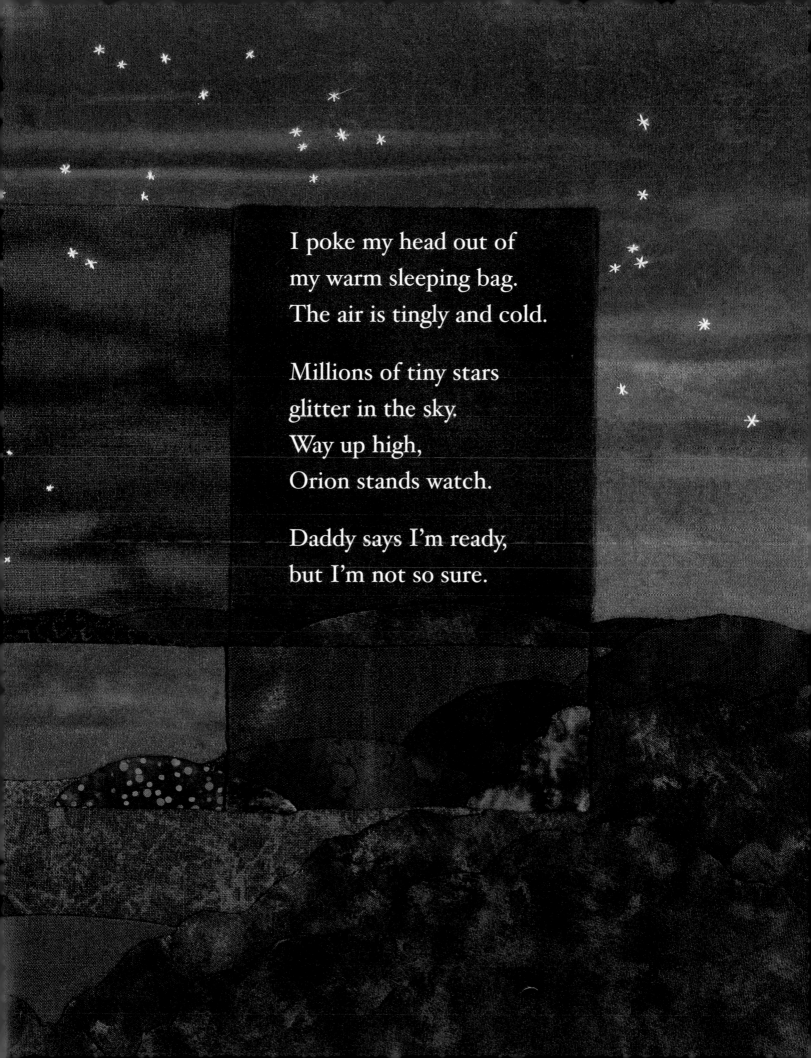

I poke my head out of
my warm sleeping bag.
The air is tingly and cold.

Millions of tiny stars
glitter in the sky.
Way up high,
Orion stands watch.

Daddy says I'm ready,
but I'm not so sure.

Daddy pushes another
branch into the fire.
Twinkling orange sparks
fly up to the stars.

"I'm ready," I whisper.
But my stomach does little flips.
Maybe I'm not.

Daddy grins at me.
"I see you're ready.
But the sun isn't."
"How long?" I ask.
"Soon," he replies.

A family of deer
peek out from the trees.
A rabbit hops by.

Soon, Daddy said.
Will I be able to?
I take in a breath and let it out,
all in a *whoosh*.

Nothing.
I knew it. Too hard.

"You can do it," Daddy says.
I tumble into his lap.
He wraps his long arms around me.

Daddy smells of smoke and
coffee, and his shirt feels
scratchy against my face.

I gulp in more air and make
my lips a tight circle
the way Daddy taught me.

Whoosh.
My breath blows away
on the wind.

"Gently," whispers Daddy.
"The way we practiced last week."

Gently.
I take in another breath,
and then
softly,
so softly,
I'm whistling.
I am!

I whistle and whistle.

A bird calls *croo-croo*.
Another answers.
And another.

The forest is full
of their sleepy songs.

"The birds are answering you,"
says Daddy.
I want to jump and shout,
but I keep whistling.

The stars fade,
and the birds sing
louder and faster.

I feel dizzy,
but I don't stop.
Not even for a second.

The last star winks and is gone.

Just when I think my lungs will burst,
Daddy's whistle starts up, rich and low.
I gulp in more air.
Together our whistling is strong and true.

The sun bursts
over the mountain peak.

I leap into the field and run
till I can't run anymore.
Then I loop back to Daddy.

"We did it," I yell.

"We whistled up the sun."

A NOTE ABOUT THE ILLUSTRATIONS

As soon as I read this story, I knew I wanted to create the pictures in fabric. Since the changing sky is so important, I wanted it to be a big feature of each page, so I designed the pictures using the landscape as my background. On top of that, I placed boxes for the text and closer views of Jake and Daddy. After searching far and wide for fabric in just the right colors and textures, I was especially happy to find Mickey Lawler's hand-painted sky fabrics.

Sewing one layer of fabric on top of another is called appliqué, a technique often used by quilters. What follows here is a step-by-step description of how I made the appliqués for this book.

—*Anna Grossnickle Hines*

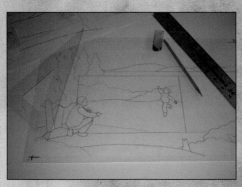

.1.

The first step is to draw the shapes exactly as I want them. I do a lot of tracing and erasing. I also use my ruler and triangle to make sure my corners are square.

.2.

With my drawing facedown on my light box, I use a fabric pen to trace the lines onto a piece of muslin fabric.

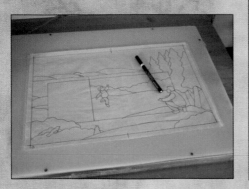

.3.

With my drawing still facedown, I trace a pattern for each piece of the picture onto freezer paper. Freezer paper has a plastic side that will stick to the fabric when pressed with a hot iron but pulls off easily when I have finished sewing the piece.

.4.

I cut out all the freezer paper patterns and lay them out like a puzzle. Now it's time for the hardest part: choosing the fabrics. I spread the other pictures out on the floor so that I can make sure the light changes gradually. I try lots of combinations before I cut any fabrics. This picture has 60 pieces to choose, cut, and sew.

.5.

I start with my fabrics organized by color and value (dark to light), but before I'm done, I have a big mess. Quilters call a collection of fabric a "stash." Since I need small bits of fabric, my stash fits in a suitcase. My remaining "mess" ends up all over my studio floor.

When I have selected a fabric, I use my iron to press the plastic side of the pattern piece to the wrong side of the fabric. I leave approximately one quarter inch of fabric around the pattern as I cut out each piece.

.6.
All the pieces are cut out, and the picture is ready to sew. Now I move over to the couch and begin the stitching, working on a plastic board on my lap.

.9.
When the appliqué is all done, I remove all the guide stitches. The last step is to add the embroidered details, such as hair, facial features, stars, and fire.

.7.
First I sew the sky, then the hills and trees in the distant background. I use a small needle and colored thread to match each fabric and carefully turn the edges under as I go.

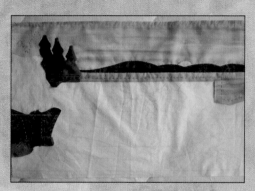

.10.
The back of the picture still shows the pen lines and many of the stitches, as well as hints of the colors. The overcast stitch all around the edges is to keep the fabric from unraveling.

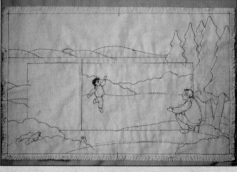

.8.
The lines I drew with the fabric pen are on the back of the muslin fabric. If they were on the front, they would soon be covered up. In order to see where to sew the next layer of pieces, I turn the work over and stitch along my pen lines, making sure that the needle goes through the layers I've already sewn on the front. When I turn the work back over, I have a line of stitches to use as a guide for placing the next layer.

.11.
Here are all sixteen interior pictures. I'm sewing them together into a quilt. It will be a very large quilt!

For my dad
—E. P.

For Jacob
and his daddy, Robert,
and
for Emmett
and his daddy, Nathan
—A. G. H.

Whistling
Text copyright © 2003 by Elizabeth Partridge
Illustrations copyright © 2003 by Anna Grossnickle Hines
All rights reserved. Manufactured in China.
www.harperchildrens.com

The handmade quilts used as illustrations in this book were reproduced
in full color. The original quilts are approximately the same size as printed.
The fabrics used by the artist to create the sky in the illustrations in this book
are Skydyes™ and were hand painted by Mickey Lawler.

The text type is Hoefler Text.

Library of Congress Cataloging-in-Publication Data

Partridge, Elizabeth.
Whistling / story by Elizabeth Partridge ; pictures by Anna Grossnickle Hines.
p.   cm.
"Greenwillow Books."
Summary: While on a camping trip with his father, a boy draws on
the whistling practice they have shared and finally whistles up the sun.
ISBN 0-06-050235-5 (trade). ISBN 0-06-050236-3 (lib. bdg.)
[1. Whistling—Fiction. 2. Fathers and sons—Fiction. 3. Camping—Fiction.]
I. Hines, Anna Grossnickle, ill. II. Title.
PZ7.P26 Wh 2003   [E]—dc21   2002023539

First Edition   10 9 8 7 6 5 4 3 2 1

Greenwillow Books